YANKEE
Doodle

★ ★ ★ ★ ★ ★ ★

GARY CHALK

DORLING KINDERSLEY

LONDON • NEW YORK • STUTTGART

A DORLING KINDERSLEY BOOK

First American Edition, 1993
10 9 8 7 6 5 4 3 2

Published in the United States by
DK Publishing, Inc., 95 Madison Avenue
New York, New York 10016

First published in Great Britain in 1993
by Dorling Kindersley Limited, London

Distributed by Houghton Mifflin Company, Boston.

Library of Congress Cataloging-in-Publication Data

Chalk, Gary.
Yankee Doodle / written and illustrated by Gary Chalk. – 1st American ed.
p.   cm.
Summary: Original verses to "Yankee Doodle" depict such events
from the American Revolution as the Boston Tea Party, Paul Revere's
ride, and the battle of Saratoga. Includes the traditional version of the song.
ISBN 1-56458-202-7
1. United States – History – Revolution, 1775-1783 – Songs and music.
2. Children's songs – United States – Texts.   [1. United States –
History – Revolution. 1775-1783 – Songs and music. 2. Songs – United
States.]   I. Title.
PZ8.3.C355Yan   1993
782.42164 – dc20   92-53482
                                                                    CIP
                                                                    AC

Reproduced by DOT Gradations Limited
Printed in Belgium by Proost

Introduction

EVERYONE KNOWS THE TUNE OF YANKEE DOODLE. It is almost a national anthem for Americans because it is so closely associated with the War of Independence, or the Revolutionary War, that brought our nation into existence.

After the "Yankees" won that war (1775-83), they formed an independent United States of America. But before the war they were British colonies, controlled by the British Army. At the beginning of the war these British "Redcoats" sometimes marched to the tune of Yankee Doodle. Any words they sang were meant to ridicule the Yankees.

Many different words were sung to this "doodle" or "tootle" that was usually played on a flute, with drums to beat out the marching rhythm. The words we know best are printed, with the tune, on the next two pages.

Generations of children have been puzzled by the "macaroni" reference in that very familiar first verse. "Macaroni" was another word for a dandy or fashionable gentleman, so it probably makes fun of the Yankees' attempts to improve their clothes. The British were a highly organized army who wore smart red uniforms. The Americans, at the beginning of the war, fought in their workclothes: many were farmers who left their fields to fight. As the war went on, they got more organized and began to wear uniforms. Some even had feathers in their caps!

The Yankee Doodle character who tootles and marches his way through the rest of the book is really the spirit of the United States. His story, of weakness turned to strength, is as uplifting as the tune of Yankee Doodle, which the Americans had adopted as their own by the end of the war.

Our version of the story is, of course, the nursery version: soldiers have popguns and hobbyhorses. And Yankee Doodle himself has a revolutionary tail!

Yankee Doodle

1. Yan-kee Doo-dle went to town A - rid-ing on a po - ny; He

stuck a feath - er in his cap, And called it mac - a - ro - ni.

Chorus

Yan - kee Doo - dle, keep it up, Yan - kee Doo - dle Dan - dy,

Mind the mu - sic and the step, And with the girls be hand - y.

2 Father and I went down to camp
Along with Captain Gooding;
There we see the men and boys
As thick as hasty pudding.

★

3 And there we see a thousand men,
As rich as Squire David;
And what they wasted every day,
I wished it could be saved.

★

4 The 'lasses they eat every day
Would keep a house a winter;
They have as much that I'll be bound
They eat it when they're a mind to.

5 And there we see a swamping gun
Large as a log of maple
Upon a deuced little cart,
A load for Father's cattle.

★

6 And every time they shoot it off
It takes a horn of powder;
It makes a noise like Father's gun,
Only a nation louder.

★

7 I went as nigh to one myself,
As Siah's underpinning;
And father went as nigh again,
I thought the deuce was in him.

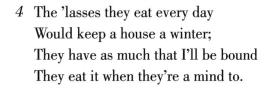

8 Cousin Simon grew so bold,
   I thought he would have cock'd it;
   It scar'd me so, I shrink'd it off,
   And hung by father's pocket.

★

9 And Captain Davis had a gun,
   He kind of clapped his hand on't,
   And stuck a crooked stabbing iron
   Upon the little end on't.

★

10 And there I see a pumpkin shell
   As big as mother's basin;
   And every time they touch'd it off,
   They scamper'd like the nation.

★

11 I see a little barrel too,
   The heads were made of leather,
   They knock'd upon't with little clubs,
   And call'd the folks together.

12 And there was Captain Washington,
   And gentlefolks about him,
   They say he's grown so tarnal proud,
   He will not ride without 'em.

★

13 He got him on his meeting clothes,
   Upon a slapping stallion,
   He set the world along in rows,
   In hundreds and in millions.

★

14 The flaming ribbons in his hat,
   They look'd so tearing fine ah,
   I wanted pockily to get,
   To give to my Jemimah.

★

15 I see another snarl of men
   A digging graves, they told me,
   So tarnal long, so tarnal deep,
   They 'tended they should hold me.

★

16 It scar'd me so, I hook'd it off,
   Nor stopp'd, as I remember,
   Nor turned about, till I got home,
   Lock'd up in mother's chamber.

It all began, it seems to me,
  With taxes set from London;
The worst was when they taxed the tea,
That's when things came all undone.

We used to like the British tea,
  But then I never drank it,
And some folks said the best thing yet
Was when the "Mohawks" sank it.

THE BOSTON TEA PARTY. A mob disguised as Mohawk Indians dumped British tea into the harbor so it wouldn't be taxed.

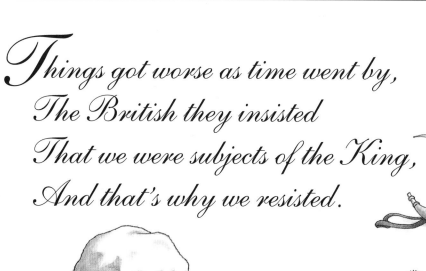

Things got worse as time went by,
The British they insisted
That we were subjects of the King,
And that's why we resisted.

Knowing that we'd have to fight,
We made our preparations:
The minutemen were ready to
Be called out to their stations.

★ The militia men, or part-time soldiers, were called "minutemen" because they had to be armed and ready in a minute. They had no uniforms, but wore their everyday clothes.

THE AMERICAN COLONISTS decided to prevent the British from seizing their arms and gunpowder. Paul Revere made a famous midnight ride to warn the militia that " The British are coming."

Redcoats were surprised to find
Us Yankees set on winning.
At Lexington a shot rang out,
It was the war's beginning!

THE AMERICANS stopped the British with
a "shot heard 'round the world"
at Lexington and Concord.

At Bunker Hill we really showed
The stuff that we were made of:
We dug a fort and fought as if
There's nothing we were 'fraid of.

THE AMERICANS dug an earthen fort on top of Bunker Hill. They were able to dig it quickly because they were used to hard work.

★ At the beginning of the war, each state had its own flag. Massachusetts had a pine tree on its flag.

★ Now the American officers had smart uniforms while their men still wore ordinary workclothes.

"We've come down with Captain Gooding. Where do you want us to dig?"

★ *"Don't fire until you see the whites of their eyes!"* William Prescott's famous command was obeyed by the Americans.

★ The battle of Bunker Hill actually took place on Breed's Hill.

ON THE FOURTH OF JULY, 1776, the Americans declared independence. They now regarded their nation as a totally separate country from Great Britain.

"We hold these truths to be self-evident; that all men are created equal; that they are endowed by their creator with certain unalienable rights; that among these are life, liberty, and the pursuit of happiness."

"Does this mean they're going to free the slaves?"

*Another year went by before
We had our declaration
Of independence which became
The creed of our whole nation.*

★ Native Americans helped both sides during the war, but especially the British.

*B*ut still we were a motley crew,
'Twas discipline we needed.
The British troops, they sure had more
Experience than we did.

1776 was very difficult for the Yankees. Well-trained British troops forced the inexperienced Americans to retreat from New York.

★ The horsemen are Britain's 17th Light Dragoons. Not many cavalry were used in the war because the country was so heavily wooded.

★ The "Don't Tread on Me" flag was one of the most common, carried by many militia units.

★ American soldiers were issued with hats and coats, but they wore all sorts of things.

"These are the times that try men's souls…"

"My soles are very tried."

During the winter of 1776, Thomas Paine wrote his famous pamphlet *The American Crisis*. He had marched with the army and shared their hardships.

WASHINGTON AND HIS TROOPS crossed the Delaware River in the depths of winter. They caught Britain's Hessian allies napping on Christmas night at Trenton.

Times were hard, the winter cold,
We really took a bruising.
But General George Washington
Was not too keen on losing.

★ The famous painting of Washington crossing the Delaware was painted in 1851 by Emanuel Leutze. In fact the Americans had no flag of their own at this point.

Every army needs a flag
To pledge unto forever,
And now we had our stars and stripes,
Red, white, and blue together.

STATES HAD THEIR OWN FLAGS and individual regiments all had at least one flag of their own. But the new country needed a special banner. The first "stars and stripes" American flag had 13 stars to represent the 13 states. They were arranged in a circle to represent "a new constellation" in a blue sky.

ACCORDING TO LEGEND, Betsy Ross was asked to make the first American flag,
using six-pointed stars, but she said five-pointed stars would look better.

Saratoga turned the tide,
The British there surrendered.

AT SARATOGA the Americans forced an entire British army to surrender to the tune
of "Yankee Doodle." The British soldiers were then shipped back to England.
They pledged not to serve again in the war against the United States.

Their uniforms in tatters now,
They didn't look so splendid.

★ The blue flag is that of the 2nd New Hampshire Regiment. A plain white flag always means "we surrender."

Winter camp at Valley Forge,
The cold was really killing,
But we became an army when
Von Steuben did the drilling.

WASHINGTON'S TROOPS went into winter quarters at Valley Forge. They were ragged and starving at first, but conditions gradually improved. A German, Baron von Steuben, drilled the troops, and turned them into a disciplined army.

★ Different regiments wore different colored uniforms.

★ Only officers could afford to buy their own uniforms.

★ Washington's aides wore blue and buff and a sash across their waistcoats.

"What a macaroni!"

Battles whether lost or won,
They each one had a story.
At Monmouth Molly Pitcher made
A name to live in glory.

AT THE BATTLE OF MONMOUTH, Molly Pitcher (wo)manned one of the guns after her husband was injured.

★ She was known as Molly Pitcher because she had carried pitchers of water to the soldiers through the heat of the day.

★ Monuments recognize her contribution to American independence, but she would not be able to share it. Women were not allowed to vote for another 142 years.

★ Cannon barrels had to be cleaned with a long-handled sponge in between shots.

Yorktown was the last big battle;
British there surrendered.
The French had helped us Yankees out,
And soon the war was ended.

British and American
artillerymen wore very similar
blue jackets. The Hessians
usually wore blue coats as well.

The American light infantry
now had smart new uniforms.

Gabions, baskets filled with
earth and stones, were used
to strengthen the earthworks.

The flag is that of the
French Gatenois Regiment.

THE FRENCH had entered the war on the
side of the Americans. Together they
forced the British and their Hessian
allies to surrender at Yorktown.

The French uniforms were
even dandier than the Yankees'!

Yankee Doodle won his war,
He seemed to be in clover.
But revolutions carried on;
Some things are never over!

"I'm going to try my
luck out west."

Yankee Doodle keep it up,
Yankee Doodle Dandy.
Mind the music and the step
And with the girls be handy!

THE WAR WAS FINALLY OVER. Yankee Doodle had become a dandy and his song was a victory celebration.

★ "The Crown" was no longer a popular tavern sign.

★ Now the British were more inclined to sing a tune called, "The World Turned Upside Down."

Some Definitions

★ *Artillery*
Big guns. Artillerymen use all types of cannon.

★ *Militia*
Ordinary people with some military training who fight as soldiers in times of emergency.

★ *Cavalry*
Soldiers who fight and move on horseback.

★ *Redcoats*
The professional soldiers of Britain's army who wore red coats as part of their uniform.

★ *Hessians*
German hired soldiers who fought on the side of the British. Most of them came from the German state of Hesse.

★ *Regiment*
A unit of an army. All soldiers in one regiment fought together. Each regiment had its own flag or flags.

★ *Infantry*
Soldiers who fight and move on foot.

★ *Yankee*
No one knows for certain where the word came from. During the Revolutionary War it was used by the British to mock the New England colonists. In the Civil War of the next century, it came to mean "Northeners." Today, in some parts of the world, the word simply means "American."